PUFFIN BOOKS

FIT WIT!

When the National Health Service reached its fortieth birthday, BBC television's *Blue Peter* came up with the idea of running a cartoon competition on the theme of keeping fit. Thousands of children from all over the country sent in their entries – some funny and some serious – to the 'Picture of Health' competition.

In this hilarious book, Puffin are proud to present the nine winning cartoons and the best runners-up. They cover the subject of health in every way you can imagine: there are cartoons on jogging and keep fit, doctors and nurses and bandages, hospitals and even injections!

All royalties from this book will be donated to NAWCH (the National Association for the Welfare of Children in Hospital).

Biddy Baxter joined the BBC as a radio Studio Manager after graduating from Durham University in 1955. She became the producer of *Listen With Mother* and BBC Schools Radio Junior English programmes and in 1961 joined BBC TV Children's Programmes, editing *Blue Peter* from 1962 to 1988.

The author of thirty-seven books, Biddy was created an MBE in 1981 and in 1988 was awarded a D.Litt. by the University of Newcastle Upon Tyne. A winner of two BAFTA Awards and the Pye Award for Distinguished Services to Television, Biddy is a passionate believer in Public Service Broadcasting. She instigated the Royal Television Society's Children's Awards and chaired the Jury from 1984–87.

A member of the Conservation Foundation, Biddy went 'independent' in August 1988. She is now writing books and working as a broadcaster and broadcasting consultant.

INTRODUCED BY H.R.H. THE PRINCE OF WALES

FIT WIT!

HUNDREDS OF CARTOONS TO MAKE YOU LAUGH AND KEEP YOU FIT!

EDITED BY BIDDY BAXTER

EMMA BECK   AGE 8   LEICESTERSHIRE

PUFFIN BOOKS

PUFFIN BOOKS
Published by the Penguin Group
27 Wrights Lane, London W8 5TZ, England
Viking Penguin Inc., 40 West 23rd Street, New York, New York 10010, USA
Penguin Books Australia Ltd, Ringwood, Victoria, Australia
Penguin Books Canada Ltd, 2801 John Street, Markham, Ontario, Canada L3R 1B4
Penguin Books (NZ) Ltd, 182–190 Wairau Road, Auckland 10, New Zealand

Penguin Books Ltd, Registered Offices: Harmondsworth, Middlesex, England

First published 1989
1 3 5 7 9 10 8 6 4 2

Cover cartoons by Guy Stanley, age 12, Foolow, South Yorkshire

Filmset in Photina
Made and printed in Great Britain by
Richard Clay Ltd, Bungay, Suffolk

CONTENTS

JAMES LEE   AGE 9   NORTH FERRIBY, HUMBERSIDE

SARAH RYAN   AGE 10   NEW OLLERTON, NOTTINGHAM

INTRODUCTION

To celebrate the fortieth anniversary of the National Health Service, *Blue Peter*, in conjunction with the King's Fund, asked children to draw or paint cartoons about keeping fit and well.

This book contains some of the best of the 16,209 entries and in addition to making you laugh – which I am sure it will – it is also helping a very good cause. All the royalties are being donated to the National Association for the Welfare of Children in Hospital.

I cannot think of a more appropriate way of celebrating forty years of the National Health Service.

Charles

JUDGING THE COMPETITION

JOANNE BRADSHAW   AGE 13   HUNTINGTON, YORKS.

That's just one of the thousands of entries for *Blue Peter*'s first-ever cartoon competition. We weren't quite sure what to expect – after all, no one younger than forty years old can remember a time when the National Health Service didn't exist, so it was a difficult idea to put over. But the results from boys and girls of all ages – the youngest was two and a half and the oldest fifteen – were far better than anyone expected. Once again *Blue Peter* viewers came up with some brilliant ideas!

First of all, there were the cartoons from people who'd either stayed in hospital or visited friends there. And although it's no joke being ill, you'd be surprised at the number of funny situations that crop up in hospital wards or operating theatres. Lots of the entries involved patients being bandaged from head to toe, with plenty of Egyptian Mummy-type jokes. There were even cartoons about something a great many people can't bear – injections. And because sport and exercise and eating the right kind of food have a lot to do with keeping healthy, they featured in some of the most hilarious of the entries.

The *Blue Peter* presenters turned up countless times, especially Mark Curry and his famous or infamous cooking! And even the animals weren't forgotten. Funniest of all was George the Tortoise winning the fitness contest. He was 99 per cent fit compared with Yvette Fielding who scored 64 per cent, Caron Keating at 59 per cent, with Mark a measly 2 per cent! You can see that on page 22, and the artist, fourteen-year-old Jackie King of Bury St Edmunds, came third in the 11s to 15s section.

But not all cartoons are funny. Sometimes they're used to make important points in an eye-catching way, and there were some excellent ones warning about the dangers of cuts in the National Health Service and praising the great achievements of the NHS.

No wonder the judges had a difficult job. As well as the *Blue Peter* presenters, they included top cartoonist Bob Godfrey, the creator of Henry's Cat, Eddie – the

Eagle – Edwards, who knows all about keeping fit, and the Chairman of the BBC, Marmaduke Hussey, who is also a member of the King's Fund, a charity specially concerned with helping hospitals and health, and whose President, the Prince of Wales, has written the introduction to this book.

All the judges were impressed by the thought and imagination that had gone into the entries and, as well as choosing the nine top prizewinners, they also selected 2,000 runners-up. There was an exhibition of some of the best cartoons at the King's Fund Centre, some were made into Christmas cards, and the very best of all are in this book.

If you're looking at the cartoons in hospital or ill in bed at home, I hope they make you laugh and let's hope *Fit Wit!* raises lots of money for a very good cause.

Biddy Baxter

THE JUDGES

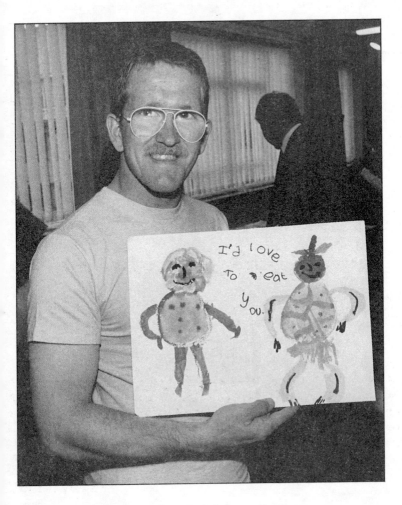

Judge Eddie – the Eagle – Edwards picks some fruit!

Judge Frank Jackson, the King's Fund's Director of Finance, organized an exhibition of the best cartoons.

The judging team. Out of the 16,209 entries, 2,000 were given runners-up awards.

A tricky decision for Mark and Yvette. To be fair, the judges voted to choose the top prizewinning cartoons.

Some of the entries were from viewers as young as two and a half. This won second prize in the 7s and Under group.

THE NINE TOP PRIZEWINNERS

THE 7s AND UNDER

ANDREW RICHARDS
AGE 7
CHIPPENHAM,
WILTSHIRE

HANNAH MOSS
AGE 4
UPMINSTER,
ESSEX

CHRISTOPHER HAMMOND
AGE 6
STOWMARKET,
SUFFOLK

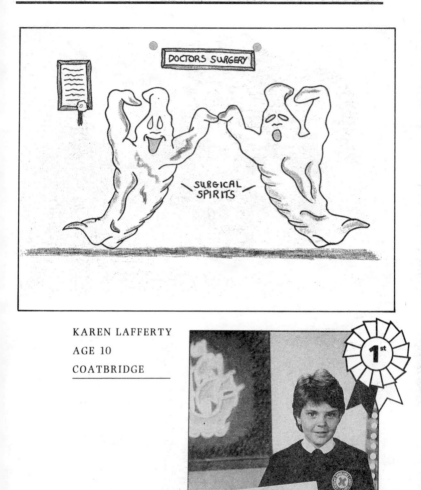

KAREN LAFFERTY
AGE 10
COATBRIDGE

BELINDA MICHELLE DAVIES
AGE 10
RHONDDA,
MID GLAMORGAN

My Grandad gets a free hearing aid. My Grandma gets free false teeth. My mother gets free glasses. My sister gets free orange juice and me? All I get is free medicine.

ANDREW SMITH
AGE 9
HESTON,
MIDDLESEX

KEVIN CORNFORD
AGE 11
SHORTGATE,
EAST SUSSEX

"I'm sure there's something a little wrong with the man in bed 3, nurse Jacobs!"

SIMON MAHER
AGE 12
SALISBURY,
WILTSHIRE

FITNESS SCORES:
CARON KEATING: 59% FIT, YVETTE FIELDING: 64% FIT,
MARK CURRY: 2% FIT, & GEORGE THE TORTOISE 99% FIT.

JACKIE KING
AGE 14
BURY ST EDMUNDS,
SUFFOLK

MUMMIES, BANDAGES AND TRACTION!

If you're reading *Fit Wit!* in hospital, these cartoons may put you off! But don't worry – the chances of anything happening to you like the patients in the next sixteen pages are highly unlikely. Being bandaged up was one of the most popular of all the cartoon ideas, so not surprisingly some of the entries were very similar. The judges compared them all and tried to pick out the jokes that had different and original touches. Some artists had obviously drawn on their own experiences. We felt very sympathetic towards the person who sent a picture of a mouse bandaged from whiskers to tail and desperate to have its ears 'itched'!

CAROLINE PREECE   AGE 14   CLEVEDON, AVON

SARAH PARSONS AGE 13 WIRRAL, MERSEYSIDE

VICKY ELLIOTT   AGE 12
MALTON, NORTH YORKSHIRE

Come on lazy bones
get out of bed and
exercise those limbs.

DAVID MARSH   AGE 10   REIGATE, SURREY

MARIA BORG   AGE 12   WIRRAL, MERSEYSIDE

LORRAINE COOK   AGE 15   HAVERHILL, SUFFOLK

CAROLINE HULLEY   AGE 10   WOODNEWTON, CAMBRIDGESHIRE

DAVID WILSON   AGE 13   SALTBURN, CLEVELAND

KERRY THOMPSON   AGE 10
DRONFIELD WOODHOUSE, S. YORKSHIRE

ROBERT GROVER   AGE 15   STOWMARKET, SUFFOLK

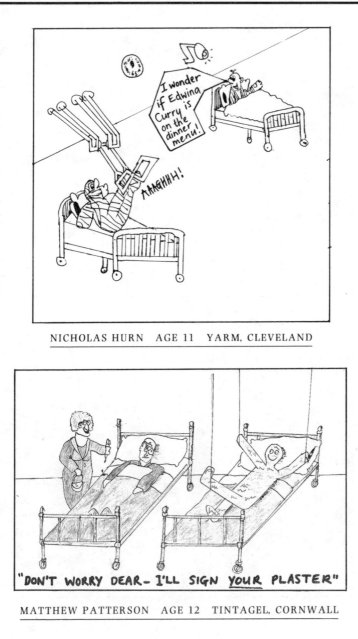

NICHOLAS HURN   AGE 11   YARM, CLEVELAND

"DON'T WORRY DEAR - I'LL SIGN _YOUR_ PLASTER"

MATTHEW PATTERSON   AGE 12   TINTAGEL, CORNWALL

ROBERT PARRY   AGE 11 SOUTHPORT, MERSEYSIDE

"He ONLY CAme iN With a Sore thumb."

HUW EVANS   AGE 7   NEWPORT, GWENT

LISA HAWKINS   AGE 14   GOSPORT, HAMPSHIRE

REBECCA MITCHELL   AGE 13   SHIPLEY, DERBYSHIRE

KARREN BEER   AGE 13   ABERGAVENNY, GWENT

"REALLY, NURSE ROBERTS, DON'T YOU KNOW WHERE THE STICKING PLASTER IS YET?!"

RUTH BESTWICK   AGE 12   TIMPERLEY, CHESHIRE

KELLY OSBORNE   AGE 9   HARDWICK, CAMBRIDGESHIRE

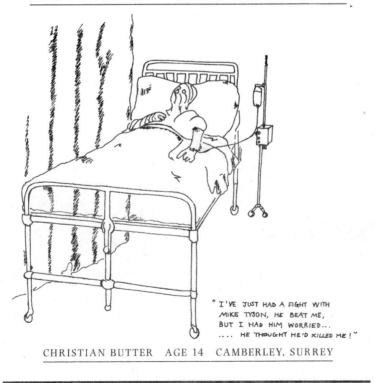

CHRISTIAN BUTTER   AGE 14   CAMBERLEY, SURREY

KEEP UP THE YOGA MR JONES.

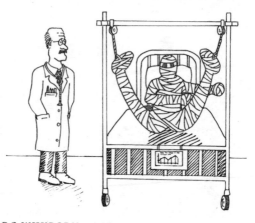

MARC WHYBORN   AGE 15   THATCHAM, BERKSHIRE

"I Want My Mummy!"

JOY RICHARDSON   AGE 10   FOLKESTONE, KENT

PENELOPE YABSLEY   AGE 14   NAILSEA, AVON

SUSAN SHIRLEY   AGE 11   BEARSDEN, GLASGOW

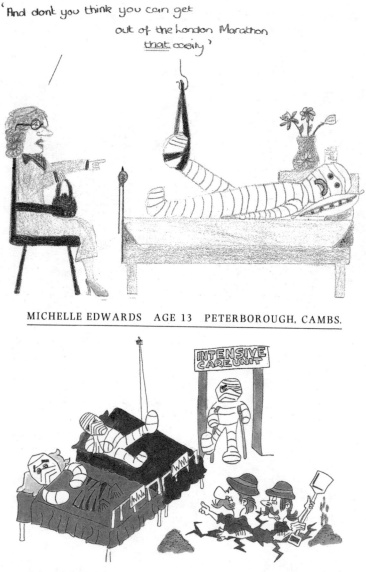

MICHELLE EDWARDS   AGE 13   PETERBOROUGH, CAMBS.

AHA! WE'VE FINALLY ARRIVED IN THE LOST PYRAMID OF THE KINGS!

MATTHEW JONES   AGE 12   BANGOR, GWYNEDD

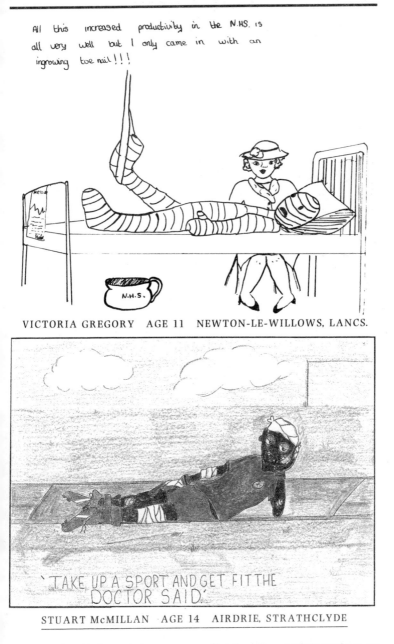

All this increased productivity in the N.H.S. is all very well but I only came in with an ingrowing toe nail !!!

VICTORIA GREGORY   AGE 11   NEWTON-LE-WILLOWS, LANCS.

'TAKE UP A SPORT AND GET FIT THE DOCTOR SAID'

STUART McMILLAN   AGE 14   AIRDRIE, STRATHCLYDE

KATE RILEY   AGE 15
ST AUSTELL, CORNWALL

CHRISTOPHER YOUNG   AGE 13   HULL, NORTHUMBERSIDE

MICHAEL YATES   AGE 14   ASHFORD, KENT

KARL MILLER   AGE 12   SOUTH BENFLEET, ESSEX

HOSPITALS, DOCTORS, NURSES AND INJECTIONS

It's very rare to come across a nasty nurse or doctor, but *Blue Peter* viewers have drawn some real dragons. And some stupid ones too – like the doctor in the operating theatre on page 49. And as for the dentist who's sneaked on to page 50, if there were a lot more like him in real life, there soon wouldn't be anyone with a full set of teeth in the country! But, without a doubt, the biggest bogy for a lot of people who entered the competition was the dreaded injection. It's lucky that in real life they're not nearly as bad as the ones shown here.

KAREN HYNTREY   AGE 7   REDCAR, CLEVELAND

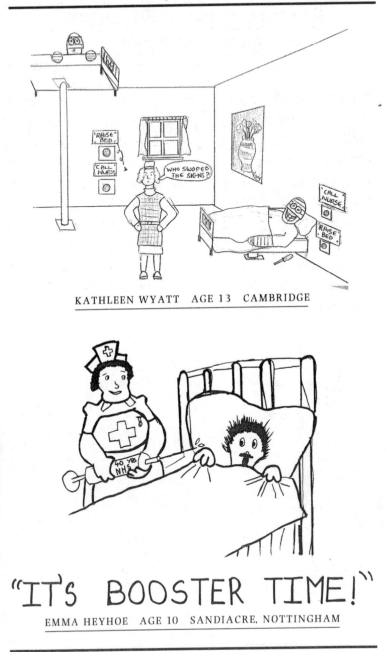

KATHLEEN WYATT   AGE 13   CAMBRIDGE

"IT'S BOOSTER TIME!"

EMMA HEYHOE   AGE 10   SANDIACRE, NOTTINGHAM

KATE STUBBS   AGE 11
TREHAMS, MID GLAMORGAN

JANE STABLES   AGE 11   WINCHESTER, HAMPSHIRE

MARY STEVENS   AGE 7   BRIGHTON, EAST SUSSEX

CAROLINE DICKENSON   AGE 10   BRENTWOOD, ESSEX

CHERYL WALES   AGE 10
SANDIACRE, NOTTINGHAMSHIRE

EMMA LOYDALL   AGE 11
MACKWORTH, DERBYSHIRE

NEIL McLAWSON   AGE 14   ICKENHAM, MIDDLESEX

RACHAEL GREGORY   AGE 15   MATLOCK, DERBYSHIRE

TOM DAHVERS   AGE 6   HEAVITREE, DEVON

SASHA CARIDIA AGE 15 BIDDENDEN, KENT

ROBIN GREENWOOD AGE 10 MONK BRETTON, S. YORKSHIRE

BARNY PHILLIPS   AGE 13   WINTERSLOW, WILTSHIRE

BEN FLETCHER   AGE 10   SLEAFORD, LINCOLNSHIRE

SIMON STEVENS   AGE 10   SOWERBY BRIDGE, W. YORKSHIRE

CAROLYN ROBINSON   AGE 6   SUTTON, SURREY

"I **KNOW** HIS APPENDIX IS HERE SOMEWHERE!"

MARK GAULTER   AGE 14   LYMINGTON, HAMPSHIRE

"EVERYONE OPEN THEIR MOUTHS – I'M GOING TO GIVE YOU YOUR MEDICINE, AND BREAK THE OLYMPIC MILE !!!! "

EMMA HIGGERSON   AGE 13   OMBERSLEY, WORCESTERSHIRE

PAULA HESFORD   AGE 13   BOLTON, GREATER MANCHESTER

ANITA DIXON   AGE 15   ERMINE WEST, LINCOLN

DARRAN WOODS   AGE 13   PORTH, MID GLAMORGAN

PHIL HARRISON   AGE 11   GORLESTON-ON-SEA, NORFOLK

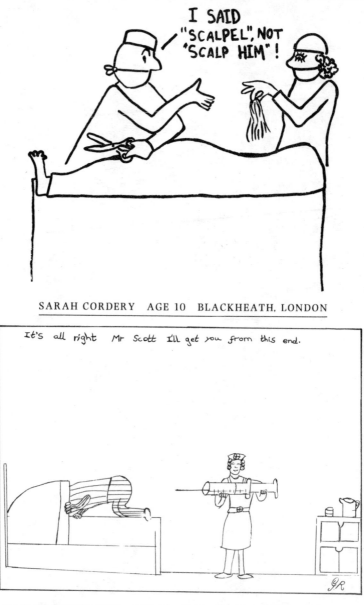

SARAH CORDERY   AGE 10   BLACKHEATH, LONDON

GILLIAN ROBERTSON   AGE 11   SUNDERLAND, TYNE AND WEAR

← HOSPITAL

I don't think he could afford that Pint of blood!

BARRY DIDCOCK   AGE 13   HORSHAM, WEST SUSSEX

GARY LEONARD   AGE 13   STONEHOUSE, STRATHCLYDE

"Anaesthetic please nurse"
"Here you are doctor"

RICHARD BARNES
AGE 10
ST ALBANS,
HERTFORDSHIRE

SEE SIR IT DIDN'T HURT A BIT.

BEN HASLER   AGE 10   NEW ASH GREEN, KENT

Hospitals are fun!

ANNA SMITH   AGE 9   BROADWINDSOR, DORSET

ANDREW JOHNSON   AGE 14   ST HELENS, MERSEYSIDE

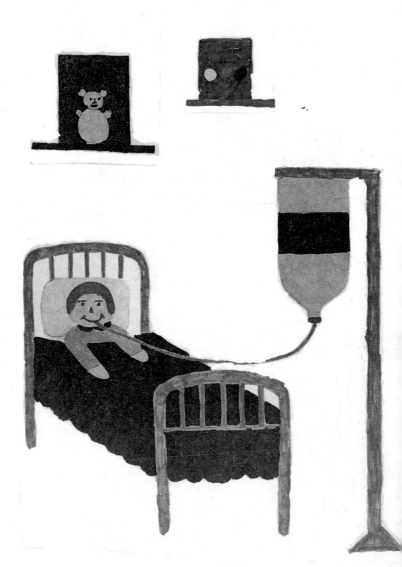

AMANDA CROFT   AGE 6   WINESTEAD, NORTH HUMBERSIDE

JACKIE NOTT   AGE 11   CREDITON, DEVON

BIANCA PEDDER   AGE 9   CHEADLE,   STAFFORDSHIRE

SALLY ROBERTS   AGE 8   BRADWELL, NORFOLK

IT WOULDN'T BE SO BAD IF HIS FATHER'S DINNER WASN'T STILL IN IT!

HELEN CLIFFORD   AGE 12   BRAMSGROVE, WORCESTERSHIRE

LYNETTE JENNISON   AGE 11   NAFFERTON, EAST YORKSHIRE

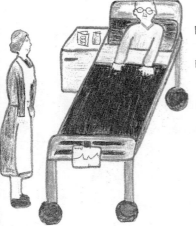

Nurse: I have some good news
and some bad news.

Patient: Can I have the bad news
first?

Nurse: You have to have a new leg.
Here's the good news.
Here's one I made earlyer with
double sided sticky tape!

ALISON PORTS   AGE 13   OFFERTON, STOCKPORT

EXERCISE

A lot of the cartoons in this section are like slogans, and very important ones too. But there's no denying that exercise has its funny side. One six-year-old viewer sent a drawing of a skeleton saying 'Do you think I've overdone the keep fit?' And the theme of how *bad* exercise can be if it's overdone, with drawings of people looking at death's door as a result, was very popular. There were several cartoons that included a member of the judges, Eddie – the Eagle – Edwards, and here's one of them.

"The Eagle Strikes Back"

MICHAEL GANN   AGE 14   TULSE HILL, LONDON

LAURA SANDERS   AGE 3
HORSHAM, WEST SUSSEX

"This jogging must be doing
me good — I've gone red in
the face."

PAUL SCHOFIELD   AGE 12   OLDHAM, LANCASHIRE

I love skipping

SAMANTHA FITTON   AGE 5   SUTTON COLDFIELD, W. MIDLANDS

JAMES SIMMONDS   AGE 15   KETTERING, NORTHAMPTON

DANIEL FOY   AGE 6   WAVERTREE, MERSEYSIDE

"Next time, I'll get somebody else to exercise the dog!"

GILLIAN MARSHALL   AGE 13   TONBRIDGE, KENT

WAYNE AVELINE   AGE 14   BENTLEY, WEST MIDLANDS

would you rather do this or put up with this?

LOUISA JONES   AGE 10   POSTHILL TAMWORTH, STAFFS.

MICHELLE MIDDLETON   AGE 11   KEIGHLEY, WEST YORKSHIRE

JOANNE NOWOGRODZKI   AGE 8   CANFORD HEATH, DORSET

CAROLINE CRAWFORD
AGE 10
COWDENBEATH, FIFE

NEVILLE WHITLEY   AGE 15   HEBBURN, TYNE AND WEAR

STUART LARKIN   AGE 12   EASTBOURNE, EAST SUSSEX

EMMA ROOKE   AGE 14   CRAWLEY, WEST SUSSEX

DEBBIE HOPE AGE 15 SUTTON, SURREY

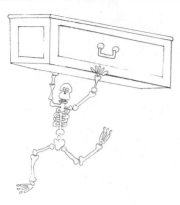

BETHAN RICHARDS   AGE 11
RHAYADER, POWYS

KEEP FIT BEFORE ITS TOO LATE

EMMA MARYNIA   AGE 9
EALING, LONDON

RUTH PROUDLOCK   AGE 7   CLEVELAND

71

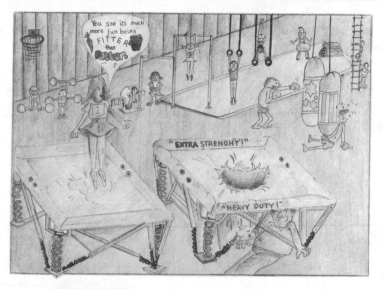

SARAH GOODARD   AGE 12   DRAYCOTT, DERBYSHIRE

IAN HUNT   AGE 11   MINEHEAD, SOMERSET

TIM ROBERTS   AGE 14
NORWICH, NORFOLK

GEORGIA BULL   AGE 6
BASINGSTOKE, HAMPSHIRE

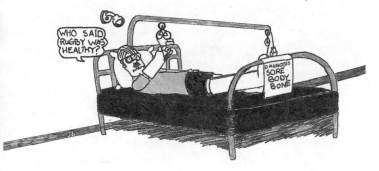

ANDREW BAILEY   AGE 12   MARYPORT, CUMBRIA

Could you show me your great long jump please?

GEMMA PAYNE   AGE 10   TORPOINT, CORNWALL

"HOW'S THAT NEW GADGET WHICH IS SUPPOSED TO MAKE YOU ALERT, FIT AND HEALTHY GETTING ON, CHAMP?"

ADAM FAIRHALL   AGE 11   LISKEARD, CORNWALL

DANIEL SKINNER   AGE 13   BARNET, HERTFORDSHIRE

keeping Fit

ADAM LANE   AGE 6
MILTON KEYNES,
BUCKINGHAMSHIRE

SUE PARKER   AGE 15
WALSALL, WEST MIDLANDS

SAVINA BOLA   AGE 7   LEICESTER, LEICESTERSHIRE

KERRY BANKS   AGE 10   BLACKPOOL, LANCASHIRE

CATHERINE ROLLS   AGE 13   WANTAGE, OXFORDSHIRE

"I BET SYLVESTER STALLONE NEVER HAD THIS MUCH TROUBLE!"

JOHN FOSTER   AGE 13   BURY ST EDMUNDS, SUFFOLK

KAREN PING   AGE 14   HARLOW, ESSEX

ALLISON IRELAND   AGE 12   ST HELENS, MERSEYSIDE

COME on 15 Miles
to go.

LEE GRANT   AGE 14   LONDON

It may look ridiculous, but it keeps you healthy

LISA PRATT   AGE 10   WEST BRIDGEFORD, NOTTINGHAMSHIRE

FIT WIT!

JULIAN JAMES BUTLER   AGE 13   BURRIDGE, HAMPSHIRE

CLAYTON MOORE   AGE 11   NORWICH, NORFOLK

SANGEETA SEHMI   AGE 14
FELTHAM, MIDDLESEX

LUKE HUNTER   AGE 7
WASHINGBORO, LINCOLNSHIRE

DEBBIE BRYANT   AGE 9   MIDDLETON, WEST YORKSHIRE

81

-"and it was supposed
to be a friendly"

STEVE HAMMOND   AGE 14   GARSTON, HERTFORDSHIRE

keep
it's on rowing —
goood for you.

MARK BIGGS   AGE 6   NORBURY, LONDON

LUCINDA DONALDSON   AGE 11   PUTNEY, LONDON

GEMMA PHILLIPS   AGE 7
CONISTON, CUMBRIA

I'm as fit as a fiddle

Do you think I've overdone the Keep fit.

GARETH JAMES McCARTHY
AGE 6   ACKWORTH,
W. YORKSHIRE

RICHARD ISAAC   AGE 14   SWANSEA, WEST GLAMORGAN

NAOMI CHIPLEN   AGE 15   WINCANTON, SOMERSET

MARK YOUNG   AGE 13   WOKING, SURREY

ADAM BAIN   AGE 13   CHERITON, KENT

CLARE SHEPPARD   AGE 14   REDHILL, SURREY

CHRISTOPHER INCLES   AGE 10   HARBOROUGH, LEICESTERSHIRE

DAVID EVANS-JONES   AGE 14   BODMIN, CORNWALL

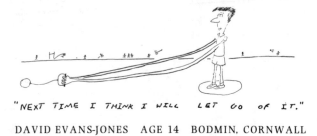

"NEXT TIME I THINK I WILL LET GO OF IT."

DAVID EVANS-JONES   AGE 14   BODMIN, CORNWALL

I'M SURE YOU WILL BE FIT ENOUGH TO TRY AGAIN NEXT YEAR MR SMITH!

KARL BRADSHAW   AGE 14   NORWICH, NORFOLK

JANE CHURCHILL   AGE 12   SHEFFIELD, SOUTH YORKSHIRE

LIZZIE EVANS-JONES   AGE 12   BODMIN, CORNWALL

"I know I said swimmings a good sport but you had to be able to swim first."

HAZEL WELLS   AGE 11   BRISTOL, AVON

I Think I Could Get To Enjoy This Keep Fit Lark After All, Roger.

JOE McCONNELL   AGE 14   STOKE-ON-TRENT, STAFFORDSHIRE

FOOD

'You are what you eat' is a famous saying, and according to one *Blue Peter* viewer, Tyrannosaurus Rex died out because he didn't eat his greens! There are some extremely ingenious ideas in this section, like the vegetable marathon on page 92 and the giant apple chasing a terrified doctor on page 103. And you couldn't have a more vivid warning of overdoing healthy eating than Lucy Philpott's idea on page 107. It gives a whole new meaning to the nickname 'carrot top'.

before   after

eat these foods to be healthy

JANCY LEE DAVIES   AGE 5   ILFRACOMBE, DEVON

KELLY LOUISE CHRISP   AGE 10   HEBBURN, TYNE AND WEAR

CLAIRE SAGE   AGE 12   RAINHAM, KENT

LAURA ANDERSON   AGE 6   CAIPLIE, FIFE

DAVID NETTLETON   AGE 13   ORPINGTON, KENT

"NO SALT PLEASE, I'M TRYING TO BE HEALTHY"

DAMION BAILEY   AGE 14
BURTON-UPON-TRENT, STAFFS.

ALEXANDER SCOTT   AGE 4
NORTHFLEET, KENT

ANTHONY MILES   AGE 9   SELLY PARK, WEST MIDLANDS

ALICIA JANE MUNCKTON   AGE 6   BARNWOOD, GLOUCS.

EDWARD BAINBRIDGE   AGE 4   DARLINGTON, COUNTY DURHAM

TOM POTTER   AGE 7   HEMEL HEMPSTEAD, HERTFORDSHIRE

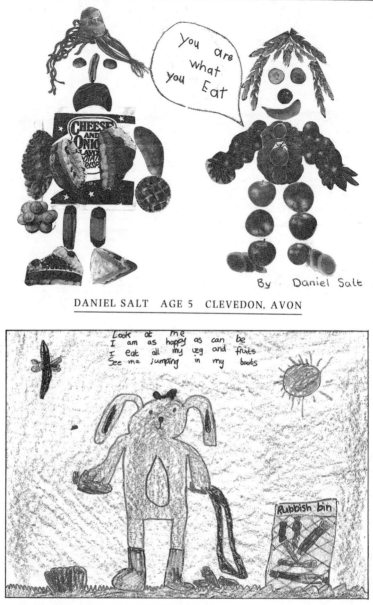

DANIEL SALT   AGE 5   CLEVEDON, AVON

KATHERINE ANN SCOTT   AGE 7   NORTHFLEET, KENT

CLARKE MAULE   AGE 12   NORTHAMPTON, NORTHAMPTONSHIRE

CARLY FROST   AGE 12   DAWLISH, DEVON

JESSIE CARYL   AGE 9   LEEDS, WEST YORKSHIRE

NEIL LETHAM   AGE 10   ALDERSHOT, HAMPSHIRE

CATHY BROCKS   AGE 9   ELBURY PARK, WORCESTERSHIRE

JAMES SALVESON   AGE 9   CAMBERLEY, SURREY

"Hello Mr. Orange, I think you had better go on a diet"

ZOË LUNNON   AGE 9   BRACKNELL, BERKSHIRE

An apple a day keeps the doctor away.

JEANETTE MARVIN   AGE 8   SHEFFIELD, SOUTH YORKSHIRE

103

HAYLEY JOHNSON   AGE 7   LEIGH-ON-SEA, ESSEX

JENNIE SMALL   AGE 8   SHEFFORD, BEDFORDSHIRE

FIONA HOUSTON   AGE 9   BRIDGE OF ALLAN, STIRLINGSHIRE

JAMES ROBINSON   AGE 9   BEBINGTON, MERSEYSIDE

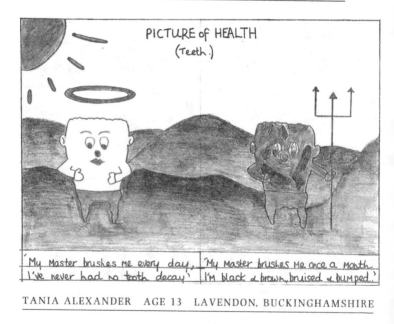

TANIA ALEXANDER   AGE 13   LAVENDON, BUCKINGHAMSHIRE

LUCY PHILPOTT   AGE 7   LEAMINGTON SPA, WARWICKSHIRE

SCOTT TAYLOR   AGE 13   BEESTON, NOTTINGHAMSHIRE

"yum yum I always knew cheese was good for me!"

ROSIE BUCK   AGE 7   BATH, AVON

SARAH PUGH   AGE 14   OSWESTRY, SHROPSHIRE

JOANNE RAYNES   AGE 14   MACCLESFIELD, CHESHIRE

MARK OSBORNE   AGE 12   LINGFIELD, SURREY

HANNAH DEMPSEY   AGE 10   ABERDEEN, GRAMPIAN

BLUE PETER

'And here's one I made earlier . . .' must be one of the most famous phrases in the English language – thanks to *Blue Peter*! Viewers certainly put it to good use in their cartoons. It turned up in bubbles over and over again, just about as often as the jokes to do with Mark's cooking. Surely his demonstrations weren't as bad as these cartoons make out? What the judges enjoyed about the keep-fit jokes with a *Blue Peter* theme was their originality – like Caron's 'weird case of dressing' on page 118 or Yvette's unfortunate accident on page 134. And on page 138 you can see a picture of health that should be very familiar to everyone who watches *Blue Peter*.

"AND HERE'S ONE I PREPARED EARLIER"

MARK DODSWORTH   AGE 14   DARLINGTON, COUNTY DURHAM

LUC EDWARDS   AGE 8   ST ALBANS, HERTFORDSHIRE

MARK POWELL   AGE 14   WIGAN, LANCASHIRE

113

MICHELLE GRIFFITHS   AGE 7   WOLSTON, COVENTRY

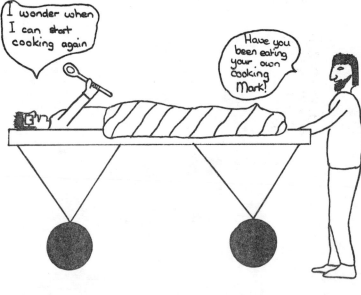

RACHEL HORNE   AGE 11   WORKSOP, NOTTINGHAMSHIRE

RICHARD ANNIS   AGE 9   BROADSTONE, DORSET

It's OK, I've Been To See Mark Curry!

JENNIFER JORY   AGE 15   REDRUTH, CORNWALL

REBECCA HODGETTS   AGE 10   EFFINGHAM, SURREY

ELLIOT MOUNTFORD HOARE   AGE 11   FYFIELD, ESSEX

GRAHAM HANCOCK   AGE 9   CLEETHORPES, HUMBERSIDE

AND HERE'S AN EXERCISE
BIKE I MADE A LITTLE EARLIER!!!

CHRIS JONES   AGE 13   HUTTON, AVON

JANELLE HOLDEN   AGE 12   CARLISLE, CUMBRIA

SUZY LACEY   AGE 11   SANDWICK, SHETLAND

SARAH WILDMAN   AGE 12   AYLESBURY, BUCKINGHAMSHIRE

REBECCA LUKINS   AGE 13   TARPORLEY, CHESHIRE

You're Looking better today Mr Curry....

LOUISE BURKS   AGE 10   LEEDS, WEST YORKSHIRE

GOVERMENT HEALTH WARNING....

MARK CURRY'S JOKES AND COOKING CAN SERIOUSLY DAMAGE YOUR HEALTH AND SANITY

GINA WOODSEY   AGE 12   GREAT BOOKHAM, SURREY

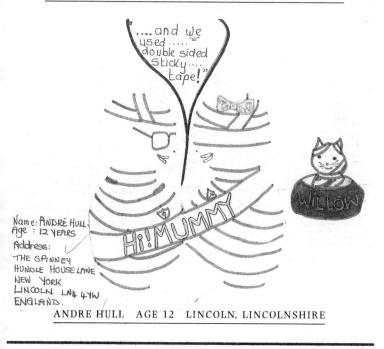

ANDRE HULL   AGE 12   LINCOLN, LINCOLNSHIRE

FIT WIT!

MICHELLE LAMBERT   AGE 13   BRISTOL, AVON

ROBERT ANSTEE   AGE 10   HEDDINGTON, WILTSHIRE

MARIE-LOUISE CRAWLEY   AGE 7   BROMSGROVE, WORCS.

"You're ill, How do you think I Feel   I am
missing Blue Peter!!!"

SALLY MOORE   AGE 12   ELLESMERE PORT, CHESHIRE

EMILY BROOKS   AGE 7   NEWPORT, ISLE OF WIGHT

MARTIN MATTHEWS   AGE 11   CROSSPOOL, SOUTH YORKSHIRE

"HOW DID I EVER GET 'ROPED' INTO DOING THIS?"

ALISON WATT   AGE 13   AUST, AVON

GARETH KNIPE   AGE 13   SUTTON COLDFIELD, WEST MIDLANDS

SUSAN SCUTT   AGE 12   WARE, HERTFORDSHIRE

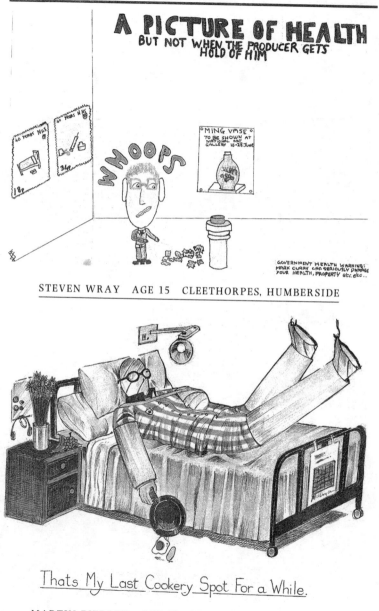

STEVEN WRAY   AGE 15   CLEETHORPES, HUMBERSIDE

That's My Last Cookery Spot For a While.

MARTIN PIERSON   AGE 15   BILLINGHAM, CLEVELAND

GEMMA TILDESLEY   AGE 10   HALESOWEN, WEST MIDLANDS

PETER BEIGHTON   AGE 14   WOLLATON PARK, NOTTS.

LULU SUREN   AGE 12   SUDBURY, SUFFOLK

KAREN NEWBOULD   AGE 13   HARROGATE, NORTH YORKSHIRE

MICHAEL DEARDEN   AGE 8   WARRINGTON, CHESHIRE

ELIZABETH HOLDER   AGE 12   SOUTH NUTFIELD, SURREY

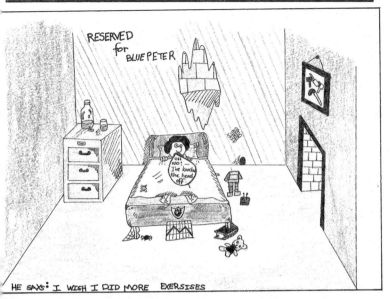

PHILIP BRELSFORD   AGE 13   DONCASTER, SOUTH YORKSHIRE

RICHARD HARRIS   AGE 14   HALESOWEN, WEST MIDLANDS

"Curry wasn't on the menu"

REBECCA DEWHURST   AGE 9   POYNTON, CHESHIRE

MATTHEW PADLEY   AGE 11   CHELTENHAM, GLOUCESTERSHIRE

AN APPLE A DAY KEEPS MARK'S COOKING AWAY! HOPEFULLY?!?

KIMBERLEY ROBB   AGE 14   KEIGHLEY, WEST YORKSHIRE

Blue Peters Keep fit class

I am puffed out

I am enjoying myself

I Hate this

Karen   Yvette   Mark

ELAINE KEW   AGE 8   ESKBANK, BORDERS

133

AMANDA GREGORY   AGE 10   LETCHWORTH, HERTFORDSHIRE

JESSICA RAWLINSON   AGE 8   BIRMINGHAM, WEST MIDLANDS

KIRSTY PENNINGTON   AGE 5   RAVENSTHORPE, NORTHANTS.

RICHARD J NORRIS   AGE 11   BARRY, SOUTH GLAMORGAN

'THAT'S NO WAY TO EXERCISE MARK'

MARCUS DAVITT   AGE 10   CHELTENHAM, GLOUCESTERSHIRE

" What do you mean, 'And what am I doing, while you're interveiwing at the London Marathon?' It's a very hard job to produce the programme!"

LUCY NEWMAN   AGE 12   COLCHESTER, ESSEX

HITESH MISTRY   AGE 13   WILLESDEN, LONDON

SHANE WOODCOCK   AGE 12   WEST EARLHAM, NORFOLK

FIT WIT!

TAKE A T-SHIRT, A PAIR OF SHORTS, A PAIR OF SOCKS, A PAIR OF TRAINERS,
A FEW THOUSAND TOILET ROLL TUBES, A CEREAL PACKET, AND STICK THEM TOGETHER
USING DOUBLE-SIDED STICKY TAPE. THEN YOU HAVE A PICTURE OF HEALTH.
WELL NEARLY.

ANDREW CONROY   AGE 12   SOUTHPORT, MERSEYSIDE

HELEN AYLETT   AGE 3   ORPINGTON, KENT

THREE CHEERS FOR THE NATIONAL HEALTH!

Before the National Health Service began, most people had to pay to go to hospital and to see a doctor. But in 1948, free medicine, hospital treatment and dental care were made available to everyone. And even though charges for medicines have been brought back, the NHS is still being described as 'the most important achievement of modern history in Britain'.

These cartoons all pay tribute to the NHS. None of the artists can remember a time when it didn't exist – let's hope it will still be there to look after their children and their children's children!

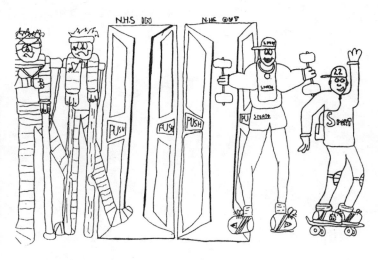

DAVID MACLEAN   AGE 7   TAYPORT, FIFE

SARAH CHANDLER   AGE 13   TRING, HERTFORDSHIRE

SARAH WOOTTON   AGE 14   LYME REGIS, DORSET

ROBERT MILBORO   AGE 7   LETCHWORTH, HERTFORDSHIRE

RHYS NICHOLAS   AGE 12   NORTH LANCING, SUSSEX

TRISTAN HADDOW-ALLEN   AGE 10   SOUTHALL, MIDDLESEX

Loadsa Service!
(Health Service)

JENNIFER EVANS   AGE 9
BOUGHTON-UNDER-BLEAN,
KENT

"WITH ALL OF THESE
NATIONAL HEALTH CUTS
I'VE GONE BACK TO
BEING THE LADY WITH
THE LAMP!!"

LUCY BATCHELOR   AGE 13   REDHILL, AVON

KATIE FLOWER   AGE 14   DRONFIELD, SOUTH YORKSHIRE

GEMMA SATTERTHWAITE   AGE 10   BLACKBURN, LANCASHIRE

SHYRLEEN WILLIAMSON   AGE 11   BIXTER, SHETLAND ISLES

Warning: SMOKING CAN SERIOUSLY DAMAGE YOUR HEALTH

TOMMY GORRELL   AGE 10   PRESTON, LANCASHIRE

ROBERT JOHNSON   MUSION FILEY, NORTH YORKSHIRE

PAUL FOX   AGE 14   BLANDFORD FORUM, DORSET

PREVENTION IS BETTER THAN QUEUE

LEAH KILLEN   AGE 11   HEMEL HEMPSTEAD, HERTFORDSHIRE

EMMA FAUNCH   AGE 14   HARLOW, ESSEX

NHS
CARING FOR
BABIES

CHUMKAR SINGH JAGPAL
AGE 10
WEST BROM,
WEST MIDLANDS

JANE McCALLUM   AGE 6   EAST KILBRIDE, GLASGOW

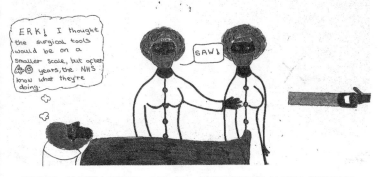

INOKA AMARAKONE   AGE 10   WORCESTER PARK, SURREY

SARAH ELLIOT   AGE 13   WANTAGE, OXFORDSHIRE

LUCY SMALLWOOD   AGE 12   UCKFIELD, EAST SUSSEX

GOOD EVENING, COULD I INTEREST YOU IN A FIRST CLASS, FREE, HEALTH SERVICE?

ALEX STANGER   AGE 12   CARLISLE, CUMBRIA

You DON'T Need wealth — TO EnJoy Good Health

BILL
OP £r
Nurse £idi
Food £b1
!
10P

1948 — 1988
40 years of the N.H.S

THERESA ANNE WALKDEN   AGE 9   HOLLINGDEAN, BRIGHTON

ANDREW DOBSON   AGE 15   BOGNOR REGIS, WEST SUSSEX

Instead of pos'session's and lots of Wealth

More important is to have happiness and good health

BARTIE WHEATLAND   AGE 11   BEXHILL-ON-SEA, EAST SUSSEX

JUDI GREEN   AGE 11   WOODCOTE, BERKSHIRE

ANNA GENNA   AGE 10   CAVERSHAM, BERKSHIRE

LEE GOLDSMITH   AGE 12   CARTERTON, OXFORD

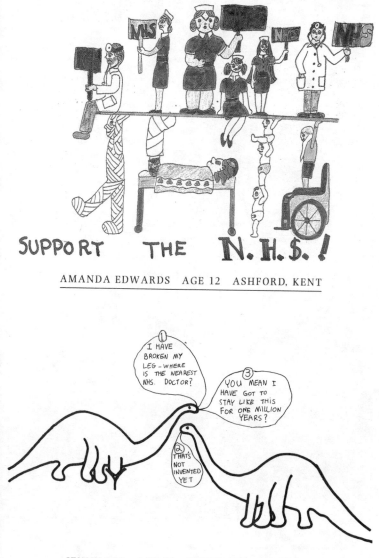

SUPPORT THE N.H.S.!

AMANDA EDWARDS   AGE 12   ASHFORD, KENT

JENNY LEE   AGE 11   SANDBACH, CHESHIRE

JENNIFER HOUNSELL   AGE 11   GREENFORD, MIDDLESEX

Thank goodness   for doctors nurses and hospitals

MOLLY BRUTON   AGE 6   BURLEIGH, GLOUCESTERSHIRE

DAVID LAIRD   AGE 12   SWINDERBY, LINCOLN

DANIEL DOWMAN
AGE 5
CHELMSFORD,
ESSEX

STUART ROBINSON   AGE 13   WEST LOTHIAN, SCOTLAND